HE'S NOT NAUGHTY!

First published in Great Britain in 2014 by Bodhi Book Press Ltd

Published in 2019
by Jessica Kingsley Publishers
73 Collier Street
London N1 9BE, UK
and
400 Market Street, Suite 400
Philadelphia, PA 19106, USA

www.jkp.com

Library of Congress Cataloging in Publication Data
A CIP catalog record for this book is available from the Library of Congress

British Library Cataloguing in Publication Data
A CIP catalogue record for this book is available from the British Library

ISBN 978 1 78592 872 7
eISBN 978 1 78592 873 4

Printed and bound in China

He's Not Naughty!

A Children's Guide to Autism

Deborah Brownson MBE

Illustrated by Ben Mason

Jessica Kingsley Publishers
London and Philadelphia

Contents

Can you spot Jake's favourite toy, 'Ted-ted'? He is hidden on every page.

Introduction

My name is Taryn (that's a girl's name by the way, it's from South Africa and means thunder!!) This is my best friend on the entire planet. His name is Jake. I am a teeny weeny bit older than him so I am the boss!

That's here

When Jake is being extra specially good like a white fluffy angel with a sparkly halo, I call him Jake. When he is being a cheeky little monkey, I call him Jacob and I make sure that I say his name, in the same way that my mum speaks to me when I am being cheeky,

"JJaaaccobb!"

and give him the, "you'd better not do that again mister," Look! I learnt it from my mummy who won a gold medal in it at the olympics!

We go everywhere together! Most people think we are twins, as we are the same height, we both have oodles of thick blonde hair, huge blue eyes and we are both super cute!!
Oh and we both love
scary dinosaurs that...

RRROOAARR!!!

ROAR!

9

Whilst we do look the Same, we don't always act the Same. Everyone Says that I am more grown up than Jake and that I behave a lot Lot better. Mummy Says that all girls grow up Faster than boys, but that's not it with Jake. His brain isn't the Same as mine, which means he can do some pretty Strange things, that can get Him into big big trouble.

I always look after him and stick up for him,

As I know that he does not do it on purpose and that it's his brain that makes him do silly things. It's not his fault, he was just born that way!

You see my friend Jake has. Autism. People with Autism are often misunderstood and mistaken for being naughty and that is really really annoying!!! Autism is a medical condition he was born with. It's not like Chicken-pox or flu or anything that makes you icky sick, but Jake will have it all his life in his brain and it affects the way he behaves and you can't make it go away with yucky sweet medicine from a big brown bottle. It's here to stay!

People with Autism see the world very differently from everyone else, which explains why they don't quite behave like everyone else. That makes them very special indeed, just like my friend Jake.

What is ASD?

ASD is like a humongous rainbow and underneath there are lots of different types of autism.

Autism Spectrum Disorder

Some say it is a hidden disability, as children with it look the same as everyone else, but can find day-to-day life much harder. No one really knows what causes ASD but they do know that it runs in families

If you look closely now at your fingertips you can see your fingerprints. Did you know that no one else in the whole wide world has a fingerprint exactly the same as yours? How cool is that? That's kind of why it's hard to understand people with autism, as every single autistic person all over the world is affected differently from everyone else. They all have their own unique autistic fingerprint.

When Granny takes me to the library, she always says that you should never judge a book by its cover and that's the same for autistic people too. They may be different than you, but they are not less than you.

If You have been asked to read
this book, then you must know
a child who has Autism.
Please take the time to get to
Know them properly.

Throw away all the rule books
on how a child should behave.
Open your mind and heart and
try to understand how scary life
can be for them.

Sensory Processing Disorder

Jake's Autism makes it hard for him to use his senses; his sight, hearing, smell, touch and taste. When I use my senses, messages are delivered to the correct part of my brain like little letters by my super quick brain postman, then my super speedy little brain works out what I am seeing or feeling and tells me what to do or say. This happens so quickly, that I don't even know that it is happening, so I feel calm and happy.

In Jake's brain, the brain Postman is very slow and makes mistakes! The message letters all get thrown around, like leaves in the wind.

which makes Jake feel like his head will explode, so he gets annoyed, screams or flaps his hands!

This makes Jake's life super hard! Because we use our senses all the time, whether we want to or not, things that are supposed to be fun, like going to the park, can make Jake really angry. If people dont understand him on top of that, telling him he's naughty then it makes it doubly hard for him.

TOUCH

The sensation meter on Jake's skin has been turned up to like a million billion.
So to Jake even a tiny little scratch from an itchy woolly jumper feels like a massive sharp sword stabbing his skin. It's unbearable!

SCRATCH

SCRATCH

SCRATCH

There are lots of unwritten rules in life, such as; when you are in public you should keep your clothes on. Jake can't pick things like this up and even if he could, he does not see why he should wear clothes if they hurt, so he just takes them off and runs around in the nude

So now, when he strips off, I just ignore the fact that I can see his winky, as it must be very horrible, if just wearing clothes hurts your skin!

I mean if your new shoes rub your heels, till it really really hurts, you would take them off wouldn't you?

How grumpy would you be if someone made you keep them on all day?!!

Hearing

Children with Autism can act like their ears don't work.

They get lost in their own world.

They don't respond when you call their name or ask them to do something.

This can make grown-ups and teachers around them Angry!

What's really happening is that.their ears are taking in so many sounds it's hard to work out what they need to listen to, so it makes life easier to ignore it all.

blah blah blah blah blah
blah blah JAKE blah blah
blah blah blah blah
blah blah blah blah
blah blah blah blah

If Jake is reading his favourite dinosaur book, you could call his name a million times with the loudest megaphone in the entire world and he wouldn't hear.

You need to get his attention before you speak to him or forget it!

When he is calm he can cut off his ears from the world. Other times, especially when he's scared, the world is SOOOOOOO loud with unexpected sudden loud horrible scary noises zooming into his ears a million miles an hour and racing around his head, bouncing off his brain, that is all too much but if Jake wears his super cool headphones they make everything.....calm again! Phew!!!

Smell

Jake has a super sensitive nose, far better than any police dog on the planet.
Smells can be so strong that they make him feel like the inside of his nose is on fire!

When there were bad smells when Jake was little, he would just scream until someone took him away from them, but when he learnt how to speak, this caused big problems!

once when a whiffy old man stood behind Jake in a supermarket queue Jake shouted to his mummy,

"That Man STINKS!"

We all know that it is rude to say that, but the smell was so overwhelming to Jake, that he couldn't help his response.

31

It is easy to shout at an autistic child for doing or saying the wrong thing, but life is so overwhelming and confusing for them. You wouldn't shout at a boy with a broken arm for not being able to juggle, would you?

Autistic children will make mistakes, help them learn and give them a break folks!!

So don't wear aftershave near Jake,
breathe on him with stinky cheesy crisp breath
or expect him to take a wee in a
smelly toilet!

33

Sight

Lots of Children with Autism won't Look you in the eye. It's too much to take in and makes them feel strange!

34

As it hurts Jake to use two senses at once, when Jake wants to listen well he looks down at the floor, so there is only one set of brain letters flying around his head!

This upsets some grown-ups, as they think he is being rude.

Sometimes children with Autism Find that the World rushes in through their eyes a million times Faster and brighter than everyone else and it Sends the brain letters into a tornado inside their brain and that HURTS!!!

This is why playing videogames for too long makes Jake have a meltdown,

which is soooo unfair as it's his favourite thing in the world to do!!

Taste

As Jake finds the world a very scary place to live in, he doesn't like any surprises when he eats.
People think he's just being fussy, but he's trying to not have a meltdown.

To keep him calm he needs to know exactly what he's eating, so he carefully checks everything before he will even think about eating it. If it doesn't look or smell the same as last time, it's not going in!

Jake has to be very brave indeed to try anything new. It can take months to do! This is because he can't bear anything fizzy or spicy, as this makes his tongue tingle which hurts and is also ultra scary as it changes the way his tongue feels.
When he eats something new he is scared it will hurt him

When Jake was small, brushing his teeth hurt so much it would make him cry. Over the years he has gotten used to it, but if you change the design of his toothpaste or the taste he won't use it!

strangers

Jake is terrified of strangers, even more so after PC Smith came into school to warn all the children about "stranger danger" and bad people trying to take children away from their mummies and Daddies.

But as Jake is soooo cute, strangers come up to him all the time and ruffle his beautiful blond hair and say things like "Well aren't you cute as a button!"

43

This is probably the worst thing you could ever do to Jake. Firstly, he will be scared as he is not at home, then someone he doesn't know at all, a stranger, who could be a bad person as they come in all shapes and sizes, has walked right up to him and without permission is touching his hair, which hurts, (if you've ever been hair sore, times it by a squillion, that's how it feels to Jake) and saying strange things to him, that don't make any sense.

44

Jake can't work out what to do or say, so he gets scared, angry and upset all at the same time, his senses blend into one causing a whirlwind of brain letters to bash around on the inside of his head all he wants is the Stranger to "go away!", so he'll shout or hit them, so they'll leave. Then people think he's being rude or naughty, which is so unfair as he was minding his own business when some stranger walked up and invaded his world.

45

So if you know a child with autism, give them their space, don't walk right up to them and ask them loads of questions, or say things that don't even make any sense and never ever touch them!

Famous People

Living with Autism isn't easy, but it's not the end of the world either.

Lots of children with Autism Spectrum Disorder have fantastically creative brains and are exceptionally gifted. If they are supported, loved and allowed to be themselves, they can make a huge difference to the world

History is jam-packed full of unique and gifted pioneers, who experts speculate may have had autism themselves; Sir Isaac Newton, Albert Einstein, Leonardo DaVinci, and William Shakespeare to name a few

It is also alleged, that two of the richest and most successful men on the planet today show signs of Autism Spectrum Disorder: Bill Gates and Mark Zuckerberg.

Bill Gates, co-founder of Microsoft, is thought to be the richest man in the world, with a net worth of 68 billion dollars. Mark Zuckerberg, the boss of Facebook, became the world's youngest billionaire at the age of 23! All of these famous people probably weren't the coolest kids in town, but went on to make a huge difference to the world! How cool is that?

Taking things literally.

Please choose your words carefully when you speak to Jake. He takes everything you say literally.
If you say, "Pull your socks up Jake!" that's exactly what he will do.

IF you say "It's Raining cats and dogs Outside" Jake will get scared as he will think dogs and cats are actually falling from the sky!

making a book containing all the Phrases that confuse Jake and explaining what they mean, Really helped!

silly Phrases and what they mean

Bullying

Sometimes Jake can have a meltdown or get really angry. Some nasty children make fun of him or call him weirdo. Sadly lots of children with Autism get bullied.

WeiRdo!

When Jake was younger he didn't notice when people were being mean but now he does and it makes him sad, as he can't help the way he was born.

I think that there should be a law against it and if you break it then you have to go to a horrible place where you are forced to eat sprouts and marmite! that would be a very stinky place to match their stinky attitudes!

feelings

Jake struggles to work out how he is feeling and it's even harder for him to tell me how he is feeling. I just know how I am feeling without even trying but Jake had to learn about feelings by using an ipad app that had lots of children's faces on it and he had to pick one that looked sad angry or happy. this is so unfair for Jake, as I just know how i am feeling, but he has to work it out and it takes a lot of effort, which makes his brain tired!

if he can't work out his own feelings then it's almost impossible for him to see how other people are feeling. this is why it's hard for him to understand how his actions make other people feel.

speech

Some children with Autism cannot speak at all, but some can still communicate with sign language, picture communication system (PECS) or speech generating iPad apps.

Teddy

When Jake was little, he'd get angry, because he couldn't say what he wanted, He'd Just point and scream a lot! A speech therapist helped him learn to speak, but he still doesn't know how to have a conversation, he just talks at you very loudly!!

People with Autism Spectrum Disorder will always find communicating with other people difficult. It doesn't come naturally to them so please be patient!

making Friends

When you find it hard to talk, it is really hard to make friends. Some children with Autism give up trying to make friends, as it never seems to work out.

I would Rather Not!

Want to be Friends?

They are often left out of games at playtime; don't get invited to parties or to play at friends houses as parents think they are naughty or other children just think they are weird.

At my school, we have a special group of people who look out for Jake when the teachers aren't around and we make sure the nasty kids can't upset him! We are...

FAKE moustaches

The BULLY POLICE!

Children with Autism make great friends as they find it hard to lie, they live in the moment, they are passionate, they don't do what's expected and life is certainly never dull when they are around!

School can be a scary place for children with Autism but they spend so much time there that choosing the right school is very importane.

If you have Autism, you can apply for an EHCP, and you might even get a lovely teaching assistant to help you to cope in class.

It's like having a school mummy or Daddy, who looks after you when your real parents aren't there.

Autism affects each child differently, so every adult and child needs to take time to get to know each child and how they need help. Why not read them this book?

Routine

Having a routine helps Jake feel safe. Any unexpected change can make him have a meltdown. Sudden changes in teachers at school can cause problems, as there is suddenly a new face, different perfume, different voice etc so Jake will switch off and not want to be there. Coping with change is something children with Autism will always need help with.

Jake loves to play the drums really loud every day! Children with Autism like to do things over and over again as it makes them feel safe and when they give all their attention to one thing, they can zone out all the confusing stuff.

This can often mean that they get really good at stuff. So when Jake is a mega superstar drummer I'll be his manager and make sure that none of the people who were nasty to him get into his concerts.

They can sit outside where it's raining cats and dogs, oops I mean where it's raining a lot!

Summary

Special children are born to special parents. People who don't understand Autism can think Jake is being naughty and that his mummy lets him do whatever he wants to do. This makes me angry as she is an awesome mummy.

72

In their kitchen, they have a painted sign saying

Those who mind don't matter, Those who matter, don't mind

Dr Seuss said that and it's true!

When you are near my friend Jake, try to talk less, smile more, be calm, keep to your routine, enjoy the present, learn from the past and leave the future to look after itself.

Deborah Brownson MBE

Forced to give up her legal career, Deborah found herself a full-time carer to her two autistic sons. Frustrated by a lack of empathy and basic understanding of this life-long condition, she wrote this book to help those around her children understand them better. Her book is now helping children, families, schools, medical professionals and businesses all over the world to better understand autistic people.

In January 2018 Deborah was awarded an MBE for her outstanding contribution to Autism Awareness. She is part of the All-Party Parliamentary Group on Autism, founder of an online autism support group, Autism Ambassador for Virgin Atlantic and advised the BBC on its drama, *The A Word*. She also works with global businesses to encourage them to employ more autistic people. She is a founder of The Autism Plan, the world's first global support platform for autism families.

Ben Mason

Ben is an illustrator from the Lake District who lives in London. Ben was diagnosed with mild Asperger's Syndrome as a child, which ensures that every illustration provides a unique visual representation of what it is truly like to have autism.

Dedicated to the real Jake,

our sunshine superstar! Love you to the moon and back!
...and to all of the misunderstood children
all over the world!